the Den

KEITH GRAY

Barrington Stoke

For my big brother, John, who taught me how to build the best dens

First published in 2023 in Great Britain by
Barrington Stoke Ltd
18 Walker Street, Edinburgh, EH3 7LP

www.barringtonstoke.co.uk

A CIP catalogue record for this book is available from the British Library upon request

ISBN: 978-1-80090-191-9

Printed by Hussar Books, Poland

CONTENTS

CHAPTER 1

Escape-Mode

I leaned right over my bike's handlebars, feeling the wind in my face. The rush of air made me scrunch up my eyes.

I rode fast, faster, fastest along the grassy track between the hedges and trees. I slammed up a gear and rammed the pedals round. I imagined I had elastic ropes, bungee cords as thick as my dad's arms, tied to my bike's seat. But if I pedalled really hard and really fast, maybe I'd stretch the cords ... Stretch them ... Snap them! And ride free.

Rory was right there with me. He was racing me, chasing me. His face was sweaty, his dark hair glued to his forehead. He was wearing his summer shorts and his legs were like skinny but powerful pistons. There was no way Rory would let me beat him.

Until he swallowed a fly.

One moment Rory was head down and pedalling hard. The next he jerked upright and made a noise like a burping dog.

Rory wobbled, his feet scuffed the ground and his handlebars twisted in his grip. He hit the hedgerow with a crash of leaves and branches. Rory tumbled over with his bike on top of him.

I didn't want to stop. I looked further up the track. But I braked and skidded, sending up a cloud of summer dust. Reluctantly I turned and rode back towards the tangle of Rory and his bike.

"You OK?" I asked.

"A bee," Rory gasped. He crawled out from under his bike and spat in the grass. "I swallowed a bee."

Every year, Rory always wore shorts, from the first day of the summer holidays until the last. Rain or shine. He was wearing his favourite pair of shorts that day. They were military green, came down to the knee, with cargo pockets. He had bloody scratches on his bare shins where the branches of the bush had clawed at him.

I was wearing jeans and the only clean T-shirt I'd been able to find. It was baggy and red.

"It was probably a fly," I told him.

"It was totally a bee, Marshall," Rory told me. "I saw it coming for me. It was *aiming* at me."

"I can't see any bees," I said.

"Because I've swallowed them all now, haven't I?" Rory replied. "I can feel it in my throat." He put his fingers in his mouth as if he could pluck it out.

I slid off my pedals, putting my feet on the ground for the first time since leaving home earlier. "Maybe it was a butterfly?" I asked.

Rory's eyes were watering. "I know a bee when I see one. It'll die now I've swallowed it, right?"

"Are you scared it's going to sting your arse on the way out?"

Rory gurgled and gobbed a green string of goz into the grass. "Tastes like crap," he said.

"Must be a fly," I said. "Bees taste of honey."

"Should I google it?" Rory asked. "I need to google it, right? Find out what happens to bees inside you."

I rocked my bike beneath me, keen to get going again.

The early morning sun looked about as round and yellow as a toddler's drawing. The sky was wide, wide open. A line of electricity pylons stretched north, cutting across the track and striding above our heads. Lazy sheep dotted the flat fields. The lonely wind turbine on Given Hill spun slow but strong.

And we couldn't see it but we could hear Crikey's Dog Hotel. Because you could always hear Crikey's Dog Hotel. It used to be an airfield and barracks for American soldiers in the Second World War. Then the buildings had been turned into kennels and were used by holiday-makers who couldn't or wouldn't take their noisy mutts away with them.

We could hear the barking even here, slapping sounds in the still air. It felt like you'd fallen off the edge of the world if you ever went anywhere and couldn't hear them.

Rory dragged the front end of his bike out of the hedge and checked his tyre for thorns. "Where we going anyway?" he said. "We could go back to mine and see if anyone's online. Sam and Trev said they'd be up for a game of—"

"Why would I want anything to do with them?" I asked.

Rory spun his wheel again, re-checking the tyre.

I'd had to twist Rory's arm into coming with me on our bikes this morning. I didn't want to be inside, trapped. I wanted to be outside, free.

"I'm in escape-mode," I said. "I just want to be as far from my house as possible."

Rory kept his eyes on his tyre as he asked, "Because of your dad?"

"Obviously," I said.

We were thirteen and had been friends for years. I was taller than Rory but he was proud that he had more muscles than me. I was skinny and wiry.

Rory knew what my dad could be like. "You all right?" he asked. He couldn't look me in the eye when he asked those kinds of questions. He stared at his spinning tyre.

"My dad's a loser," I said. I'd dodged a proper answer but still made Rory look even more uncomfortable. I kicked my bike's pedals round and round. "I just think that it's the first day of the summer holidays, so I reckon we should do something new and amazing and different."

Rory got back on his bike. "You know there's been nothing new or different around here since the Jurassic Period? And we both know the problem with living in the middle of nowhere is that there's nowhere to go."

I shrugged.

Rory shrugged too.

Then he said, "What about seeing what's been done to Skelter Cottage?"

"We've been there a million times," I said, unimpressed.

"Not for ages," Rory said. "Not since last summer."

Skelter Cottage was an abandoned and broken-down house on the edge of the woods. It was where we used to dare each other to play as little kids because everyone reckoned it was a hundred years old and haunted. Even so, it was true that it'd been ages since we'd bothered going that far on our bikes.

"It's been knocked down," Rory said.

"Knocked down?"

"That's what I heard," Rory said. "Total bulldozer carnage!"

Maybe I thought haunted houses sounded silly and childish these days but somehow I liked the sound of *total bulldozer carnage*. Also, it would take us at least half an hour to ride to Skelter Woods and I reckoned any time further away from home sounded like a good idea.

CHAPTER 2
The Trapdoor

Rory had been wrong. Skelter Cottage wasn't carnage. This was as if our childhood "haunted house" had never even existed. Truck and bulldozer tracks were crushed into the grey-brown mud leading up to a small scattering of rubble. Where the cottage used to stand was now mostly bare ground under the trees at the edge of the woods. It was as if Skelter Cottage had been picked up in a massive bucket and carried away.

Rory dropped his bike on its side. "Where's it all gone?" he said.

There were glinting puddles of smashed glass, a few broken bricks and a couple of uprooted pipes. There was a mound of filthy lino that had curled up on itself and a cluster of wire flex sprouting from the ground like weird weeds.

Rory's disappointment dragged on his face. "I thought it was going to look like one of those bomb sites you see in war movies."

"Me too," I said.

I laid down my bike next to Rory's. The cottage's shape could still be seen – there were faint straight lines and square angles across the dry ground where the walls used to stand. I walked along these lines, tracing the old building's foundations, trying to remember how the cottage had looked.

"This is where the kitchen was, right?" I asked.

Rory ran over and jumped into the middle of what was once a room. "I'm in the living room," he said. "Told you I dared go in further than you."

When it had been standing, the windows had all been smashed and the front door knocked down, and everything was boarded up. But someone had battered open a gap in the kitchen window. That was how we used to climb inside.

The cottage had always been pitch-black inside, even in the middle of the day. And we'd only ever dared go as far as the kitchen back then because we'd been nervy little kids who still believed in ghosts. But if you felt brave and peered through the kitchen door into the next room, you could see dropped tab ends and crushed beer cans, which proved the older kids were even braver.

"Hey, Marshall. Where do you reckon all the ghosts who lived here went?" Rory called. He wandered over to the edge of the trees, scuffing his feet all the way.

"I wish we'd been here to see the bulldozers," I said.

Rory didn't answer. He was on his hands and knees, prodding and poking at something on the ground.

"What is it?" I asked.

He shook his head. "Don't know." Rory started digging with his fingers, pulling up lumps of mud. "Could be a handle."

I went over and crouched next to him. The sun was still strong even under the trees. Rory was tugging on a thick metal ring that was stuck in the hard mud.

"Maybe it's a trapdoor or something," he said.

"It won't be," I said. Even so, I started scraping at the hard mud too. We found a red-brown metal sheet, maybe a metre by a metre, half buried in the ground. "It's not a trapdoor."

But as we dug away even more mud we saw I was wrong.

And we swore with surprise and excitement.

I grabbed the nearest fallen branch and used it to dig at the packed earth around the trapdoor's edges. At the opposite end to the ring-handle I found rusty hinges.

"It'll just be a coal bunker," I said. But I hoped it was going to be so much more.

"I never knew there was a coal bunker here," Rory said. "Did you? I bet nobody did. I bet it's been secret for years, centuries, *millennia*. And hidden right under the cottage all the time."

Rory stood up and prodded the metal trapdoor with the toe of his trainer. Then kicked it. Then stamped on it as hard as he could.

We both jumped back but the trapdoor didn't crack or collapse. It just made the sound of a crap bell.

"Open it together?" Rory asked.

We took hold of the ring-handle. It was difficult for us both to get a proper grip at the same time and the trapdoor wasn't budging. So we scraped even more chunks of mud away from the edges. Then we slid the branch through the ring-handle and took one end each. We gripped it while standing each side, and heaved. But the trapdoor was stuck, jammed.

"Come on, come on," Rory grunted.

We tried again with the branch, using all of our strength together. We huffed and groaned and gritted our teeth.

The trapdoor's hinges squeaked and cracked. It swung up, back and open with a gruff breath. Pebbles and mud fell away from around the edges, pattering down onto an unseen floor in the darkness below.

We were sweating again. The sun felt hotter than ever. We got down on our bellies to peer into the black hole we'd discovered.

I looked at Rory. Rory looked at me.

"You first," we said at the exact same time.

CHAPTER 3

The World's Most Amazing Secret

It felt like we'd discovered the world's most amazing secret.

"We've got to go in," Rory said. "I can't imagine *not* going in. I want to know what's down there. You want to know what's down there too, right? I mean, I'd always be thinking about it for ever if I never knew, wouldn't I?"

"Get your bike light," I told Rory. "The front one."

He hurried over to where we'd left our bikes.

It was true I'd never dared go into the cottage's dark rooms beyond the kitchen when I was a kid. But I'd decided to stop believing in ghosts when I was ten. I was excited to explore what was down there.

Rory ran back with his front bike light, clicking it on and off to make sure the battery was

OK. The dark, square hole below us smelled musty, stuffy – as if a room could have morning breath.

We waited and listened but all we could hear was the faint barking from Crikey's Dog Hotel.

Rory got down on his hands and knees again. "Do you reckon we should arm ourselves?"

"What?" I said.

"Get some weapons," Rory said. "Just in case. Might be that some badass axeman murderer lives down there."

"As if," I sneered.

"You say that but how do you know?"

"How could anyone survive stuck down there for years and years?" I asked. "The trapdoor was all sealed up."

"Doesn't mean it's not dangerous. We should google it," Rory said.

"What?"

"We should google Skelter Cottage and see what it says." Rory already had his phone out.

I laughed. "If it's got a wiki page, I'll give you ten thousand pounds."

"You don't even have ten thousand pounds," Rory said.

"Bet me and find out."

Rory knew I didn't have any money at all. He shoved his phone back in his pocket. "I suppose if nobody knows about this place, then it can't have a wiki page, can it?" he said.

"Exactly," I agreed.

I squirmed on my belly as far over the edge of the square hole as I could. I ducked my head down, holding the bike light out in front of me. I didn't think the room down there was much bigger than my bedroom but the light didn't have the power to shine into all the corners. I could see the glimmer of pale walls but not much else.

"Are there coffins?" Rory asked. "It's a crypt, right?"

"Could be a bomb shelter," I said. "From World War Two. Maybe whoever built it didn't like being too near to Crikey's when it was still an airfield full of American soldiers."

We listened to the barking again – always sounding closer than it really was.

Rory leaned over the hole. "How do we get in?" he said.

I stretched down as far as I could with the bike light. The sudden crashing, thudding, squealing, screaming noise surprised me so much I almost toppled in head-first. I yelped and scuttled backwards.

"Sorry," Rory said. "My phone. Sorry."

We had a long-running competition between us to see who dared have the loudest and most annoying ringtone. Rory was winning so far because he'd discovered a heavy metal band called Napalm Death and downloaded one of their songs for his phone. It sounded doubly terrible in this clearing at the edge of the calm woods on a summer's day.

"It's my mum calling," Rory said. "She'll want me to come home."

"Don't answer it then," I said. "You want to see what's down here first, don't you?"

Rory shrugged, nodded and rejected the call, but he looked worried doing it.

I leaned down into the trapdoor again. "There's a ladder on the floor."

"No use to us down there," Rory said.

"Means we can get out again," I replied.

"Maybe. But what if it's broken or snapped? And that's why nobody could get out alive. And that's why they all died trapped down there."

"Who are you talking about?" I said. "How do you know the ladder didn't just fall over? Maybe the bulldozers driving around up here shook the ground so much it fell down."

"Or maybe whoever was last to climb out kicked it over so nobody else could ever get in ever again. Because it's cursed and haunted down there."

"Get a grip," I told Rory. "It's not that high, or deep, or whatever. Not that far down. We can hang and drop."

I turned and shuffled backwards to let my feet dangle down into the hole. But the ground was dry mud – loose crumbly chunks with nothing to hold on to. My weight took me as my legs, hips and belly slid over the edge.

"Marshall! Watch out!" Rory said, too late.

I slipped down into the darkness faster than a hot dog down a greedy kid's throat.

CHAPTER 4

Down Inside

I landed on my feet, jarring my knees and rattling my balls. I staggered, windmilled my arms, but managed to stay upright.

I'd kicked up cloudy dust and it hung in the shaft of sunlight from the hole above. I reckoned I was the first person to disturb this place in years and years and years. After the heat of the summer sun up there, the sudden coolness down here made me tingle with instant goosebumps.

"Marshall?" Rory leaned over the hole as far as he dared and asked, "Is it safe?"

"I've not been attacked by any badass axeman murderers if that's what you mean," I replied. Yet as I said it I shone the bike light behind me. Just in case. Then I turned and flashed it the other way too.

The chair surprised me. In the middle of the floor was a once-plump armchair now looking rat-gnawed and saggy. It looked like someone had been sitting there alone in the dark staring up at the trapdoor, waiting all these years. The thought brought bigger goosebumps and I rubbed my arms to get rid of them.

"What can you see?" Rory asked.

"A chair," I said. "But no one's sitting in it."

"Anything else?"

"Why don't you come down and look yourself?"

Everything beyond the trapdoor's shaft of sunlight was murky darkness. The bike light's beam was too weak to see all four walls at once.

The ladder on the ground looked ancient. I got splinters in my hands as I struggled to move it into position below the trapdoor. Rory reached down to grab it and we managed to rest it against the edge of the hole.

"You coming down or what?" I called. "Because you'll never know what's in here and always be thinking about it for ever if you don't, right?"

Rory took his time. He tested the ladder with one foot first, putting his weight on it. When it didn't snap or crack, he risked his second foot. Then he scuttled down in a rush.

"Don't walk off with the light!" Rory whined.

"How else can I see what's down here?" I said.

"What's to see? Even the cobwebs have been abandoned. It's like that boat down here."

"The *Titanic*?" I said.

"No, that one sank," Rory replied. "What's that other one called that everyone disappeared from?"

I didn't have a clue what he was on about.

"I'll google it," Rory said.

I moved away from the beam of sunlight falling through the trapdoor. Rory could follow me if he wanted to. I poked the bike light at patches of darkness. The walls were mud and stone. There were two thick wooden pillars against the walls on both sides. These supported two massive overhead beams that held up the roof – or the ground, depending on your point of view.

"That looks bad," Rory said. He pointed at the wooden beam right above us.

Even in the dim light, the jagged, splintered crack in the wood was easy to see.

"I guess the beams weren't meant to hold up the weight of bulldozers and trucks as well as the actual cottage," I said. "But it proves how strong it is if everything hasn't all collapsed already. It had to be strong if it was a bomb shelter, right?"

How was I to know if the roof was likely to cave in on us? I suppose I was convincing myself that it wouldn't as much as Rory.

"I still don't get why nobody knows it's here," he said.

"When was the last time anybody needed a bomb shelter?" I said. "Eighty years ago? It just got abandoned like the cottage and no one was around to remember it any more."

Rory shrugged, nodded. "Why are you whispering?" he asked.

"Because you are," I told him.

I shone the bike light on a wonky bookcase that was leaning against the wall on our left. It was wonky because of the uneven ground. The shelves were covered in shabby, dusty cobwebs. On top were two dirty saucers overflowing with the hard dribbles and solid splotches of melted candles. On the shelf below was a red-and-green cardboard box about the same size as the box my phone had come in. Past the eighty-year-old layer of grime on the box front we could read the words "ELEY REX CARTRIDGES – 12 Gauge".

"Bullets," Rory gasped. He snatched the box up. But shrugged when he saw it was empty.

"Do you reckon maybe the gun's down here too?" Rory asked. He squinted around as if he'd see the shotgun glowing in the dark somewhere. On the back of the box it read "KEEP OUT OF REACH OF CHILDREN". So I took it off Rory, put it back on the shelf.

There was a pile of toppled chess pieces on the shelf below but no chessboard, and a row of tattered books. The books looked like they might crumble and flake apart if you touched them.

Rory tilted his head to read the titles on the spines but wasn't impressed. "It's the kind of stuff we get forced to read at school."

"Seen the movies," I said.

On the next shelf down was an old-fashioned pair of glasses with round lenses. The kind of glasses made of thin wire with arms that curled all the way behind your ears. One of the lenses was cracked. There was also a silver photo frame that looked like something a proud granny might keep with a picture of her family inside. But the frame was empty, so gave us no clue as to who needed a shotgun when they played chess and read boring books.

We moved away from the bookcase towards the far end, which I reckoned was below where the kitchen used to be. There was a metal-frame bed pushed up against the wall. It still had a mattress that was as dusty and dirty as everything else but down the middle was a saggy person-sized dent. You could almost see the shape of the shoulder and curve of the back of the person who'd curled up there to sleep. Someone had spent many nights down here.

I gave Rory a sideways glance, wondering if he was going to freak out.

"It's old, right?" he said. "Just tell me it's old and no one's actually slept here for years and years and years."

"At least eighty," I reminded him.

"That's OK then." Rory nodded. "I can deal with that."

I wondered if I should be feeling more freaked out. I had two voices in my head, both talking at once. One voice said, *Spooky place this. Maybe dangerous. Why are you so interested?* But the second voice whispered, *Because it's secret. Because no one knows about it. And if me and Rory keep our mouths shut, no one else will ever find out.*

I stood still and listened. "Can you hear that?" I asked Rory.

He was worried. "What? Hear what?"

"Nothing," I said.

"Very funny," Rory groaned.

But I wasn't joking. It was silent. I couldn't even hear the barking from Crikey's dogs down here.

"What's that?" Rory asked.

He was talking about a bulky shape in the shadows against the far wall. It turned out to be a large wooden chest. It almost looked like something a pirate might bury on a treasure island.

"You could fit a dead body in there," Rory said. "I dare you to open it."

"Why don't you open it?" I asked.

"Because I dared you first." Rory looked nervous as I reached out to lift the lid and he took three steps back towards the ladder. "Tell me if it's a skeleton," he said.

The chest was full of neatly folded woollen blankets.

"Total anti-climax," Rory complained.

A sudden screaming, squealing noise shocked us both so much we ran for the ladder. The noise crashed and echoed off the walls around us. Rory was up the ladder and outside faster than a supersonic monkey with his arse on fire. And only then did he realise what the noise was.

He poked his head down into the trapdoor looking embarrassed. "It's my mum," Rory said. He waved his phone at me. "She wants me to go home. Are you coming?"

I climbed up the ladder slowly. Really, really slowly.

First day of the holidays and we'd discovered something amazing. And I was already making amazing plans in my head for the rest of the summer.

This place was going to be mine.

My den. My hideout. My escape.

CHAPTER 5

The Dare

Rory had to go home. He wasn't happy about it.

"It's day one of the holidays and my mum's already wanting me to do stuff for her." Rory squeezed his phone in both hands, pretending to strangle it. "I bet she looks forward to school holidays just so she can have me at home to boss around all the time, doing everything for her."

I stayed quiet. I was far from being any kind of expert when it came to parents.

"Come with me if you want," Rory said. "We can get my mum's jobs done faster together. And I said I'd meet Sam and Trev online for a game later."

"I'd rather punch myself in the face," I said. It was almost a joke. Or maybe half a joke. Because the last time I'd talked to Trev, he'd punched me in the face. It had happened in the Easter holidays.

"Are you just gonna try to dodge them all summer?" Rory asked.

I nodded. "That's the plan. And don't tell them about this," I said, pointing at the trapdoor. "I mean it. We found it. It's ours, OK?"

Rory shrugged and said, "OK."

"I mean it, Rory. No way do I want them hanging around here."

"I said OK, didn't I?"

"I'm dead serious," I said, and grabbed the front of his T-shirt.

"I know, Marshall. I know. I heard you." Rory brushed my hand away.

"Are you coming back?" I asked. "I want to get a proper torch. Something stronger than this anyway." I handed him his bike light. "And a screwdriver so we can take the trapdoor handle off. It's what you saw first, right? People walk their dogs in the woods and along the farm track, so anyone might see it."

"Let's come back tomorrow," Rory said.

"I think us finding it is the best thing that's ever happened around here," I said.

"Yeah, me too," Rory agreed. "Even if loads of people probably died down there."

Reluctantly I let the trapdoor fall into place with a *whoomf* of dusty earth. Rory helped me wedge chunks of mud around the edges and we stamped them down, trying to cover up what we'd dug away. We sprinkled the top with dirt and scattered it around with our hands. I grabbed a couple of small branches and dropped them on top too, hiding the handle.

"We've got to keep it secret," I said. "It's our den, OK? Agreed? Nobody else's."

Rory nodded.

We picked up our bikes and climbed on. The trapdoor was magnetic to me – I couldn't stop looking at it. I had to tell myself that it was in the shadow of the trees, that we'd hidden it again, and that no one was going to come looking anyway because no one ever came here any more.

"Do you reckon we dare stay overnight?" I asked.

"What? Down inside?" Rory was surprised. But he said, "I dare if you do."

"Tonight," I said.

Rory hesitated but said, "OK."

"You'd better not chicken out."

"*You'd* better not chicken out."

CHAPTER 6

Dad's Hands

Rory and I went different ways when we got back to the village. I wanted to look for a torch, so I headed straight home. My house was down a cul-de-sac. Or dead end. It depended on your point of view. And ours was the scruffy house on the far side.

I hopped my bike up onto the pavement, freewheeling at speed past the broken garden gate. Dad was home. I could hear his music blaring out. He loved old-fashioned heavy rock stuff. AC/DC, Ozzy Osbourne, Iron Maiden. Stuff that a lot of the kids at school had never even heard of. My stomach twisted up like someone had grabbed my insides in a cold fist. I dropped my bike in the long grass of our front garden but hesitated before I went into the house.

I needed Dad to be in a good mood if I was going to ask about staying out all night. I hoped he was in a better mood than yesterday. One minute Dad had been shouting, the next crying. And no matter what I'd tried to do to help, I'd always been in the wrong. I'd made his coffee too weak, Dad said. He was sick and tired of frozen pizza for dinner, Dad said. I'd stayed in my bedroom, keeping well out of his way.

I shouted I was home as I walked through the front door. Even above the music, I heard a chair scrape on the kitchen floor. I walked into the kitchen and Dad was standing at the sink with his back to me, up to his elbows in dirty dishes. He was wearing a grey T-shirt and faded jeans with bare feet. His long hair was in a straggly, greasy ponytail.

On the kitchen table was a small plastic bottle of painkillers, a half-drunk mug of black coffee and an ashtray holding a half-smoked cigarette. His guitar was leaning against the table and I thought that might be a good sign. Maybe he'd been playing it again?

At last Dad glanced backwards and flashed a wide smile at me. "Hey there, Marshall," he shouted over the music. "Cool. You're home. Didn't hear you come in."

"It's hot in here," I said. It smelled of sour sweat and stale smoke.

"I've already had Half-Dead Harold from next door mouthing off about my music being too loud, so I closed all the windows," Dad said.

He dried his crooked hands on the hem of the T-shirt he was wearing, then reached up to the old-fashioned portable stereo on the shelf. It was one that played CDs. Dad turned the volume down a couple of notches. Just low enough that our neighbours wouldn't be able to hear it.

I pushed the window as wide as it would go. And I couldn't help thinking, *Escape route*. Which was silly. Just a joke ...

"Come on and finish up here for me, pal, would you?" Dad said, pointing at the dishes in the sink. "Honest to God, I've been tidying up all morning. Your sister called to say she's coming over and I don't want her thinking we live worse than Crikey's dogs, do I?"

I did as Dad asked. There was nearly a week's worth of dishes, the water was cold and the Fairy Liquid bubbles were flat. But knowing Laney was going to visit was brilliant news.

"When's she coming?" I asked. "Is she staying over?"

Dad sat down at the table and took the glowing cigarette from the ashtray with his twisted fingers. "She'll turn up," he said, "tell me everything that's wrong with me, then go again. Same old, same old." Dad picked up his guitar and cradled it in his lap but didn't try to play it.

I'd never touched his guitar. Never dared. But I'd never wanted to either.

"Did Laney say anything about Mum?" I asked.

Dad ignored me. And I didn't have the guts to ask a second time. I wondered if he'd pluck a note or even strum a chord on his guitar. But he just sat there with it in his lap, smoking. Same as always.

When I'd been little, Dad hadn't been around much. Back then his job had been a roadie for rock bands on tour. He'd hauled musical instruments and amplifier equipment in and out of boozy nightclubs and dingy halls, setting up concerts all over Europe. Dad had loved it. And he'd always brought home tour T-shirts for me and Laney that were emblazoned with the logo of whichever band he'd been travelling with.

He'd tell us about the cities listed on the T-shirt's back, cities he'd visited, telling us stories from Copenhagen, Düsseldorf, Vienna, Budapest. Dad used to make the city names sound other-worldly, even a bit like Narnia. We'd never been allowed to wear the T-shirts and these days they were folded away in boxes upstairs. I knew Dad took them out to look at sometimes.

Dad had only ever wanted to be the guitarist in a rock band of his own since he'd been a kid himself. As a roadie, he'd got a kick out of hanging around and being friends with musicians. Until one night when a lighting rig above the stage had collapsed.

Dad had been dismantling it after the show, got his hands in awkward places, and a ton of heavy metal scaffolding had crashed down. He'd broken every bone in both hands.

Dad liked to tell people, "My screaming could've blown the speakers. I was louder than the band could ever dream of being."

Across his palms were thick, ugly scars. Dad sometimes held them up and joked, "Any fortune teller's gonna have a fit trying to read these."

Dad's hands still ached and cramped. He'd tell anyone who'd listen that he could have, would have, should have been a famous guitarist. He'd even named me and my older sister after his favourite makes of guitar amplifier, Laney and Marshall. We used to think it was funny to shout a lot as little kids, to try to live up to our names. But nowadays all Dad did was listen to his old CDs, drink coffee, smoke and take lots of painkillers. He carried his guitar from room to room yet never played it. He worked at Crikey's Dog Hotel. He said he liked the dogs but couldn't stand their owners.

Mum left five years ago when I was eight. I video-called with her twice a week and it was always awkward because I never knew what to say. I sat there in silence while she talked at me.

Laney had gone to Lincoln University three years ago. When she came back to visit, she never stayed longer than a night or two. I wasn't clever enough to go to uni like her. So I had to figure out other ways to escape.

Dad puffed on his cigarette. "You were out early this morning." He had to raise his voice to be heard above his music. "Where you been?"

"Just out with Rory on our bikes," I said.

"What? Can't hear you," Dad said.

"Out with Rory," I repeated. "Then his mum called and he had to go home." It was half the truth.

Dad laughed. "Aren't you glad your old man's not a nag like she is? Poor Rory, right?"

I stayed quiet as I rinsed the dishes. I knew I needed to keep him in a good mood – which wasn't always easy. I sometimes thought it was lucky I was so skinny because I was always walking on eggshells around him.

I'd finished all of the washing-up by the time I'd plucked up the courage to ask, "Would it be OK if me and Rory camped out tonight?"

"You reckon his mum will let him?" Dad sneered.

"She's already said yes," I replied. I guessed Dad wouldn't want to say no if he thought he'd look bad or uncool compared to Rory's mum.

And I was right. "Makes no difference to me," Dad said, blowing smoke, staring at his guitar in his lap. "They've got a tent, have they?"

"Yeah, but do we have a torch we can use?" I asked.

Dad shrugged. "If we do, it'll be in the garden shed."

"I'll go look."

"Why don't you invite the Crikey lad to go with you?" Dad said.

That surprised me. "What? Greg?" I avoided Greg at school. *Everybody* avoided Greg at school. He always had dog turds squished into the soles of his shoes.

Dad nodded. "When Greg's not at school, all the lad does is sit on the internet all the time playing games. So his old man tells me."

I almost pointed out that that was what most kids did these days. And the only reason I didn't was because I hated being at home.

"His old man's my boss," Dad went on. "I said I'd get you to call round for Greg sometime. I reckon he could join in with you and your mates, right?"

No way was I going to tell Greg Crikey about the den.

"Where are you planning on camping anyway?" Dad asked.

“Rory’s back garden,” I lied. “And I don’t even know if the tent could fit three of us.”

Dad wasn’t impressed. “Do you know what we used to do when we was your age?” he said. “We’d spend the night in Skelter Cottage.”

The shock on my face was real. It was sudden worry that he’d somehow guessed where I’d been that morning and what I was planning tonight. But I realised Dad thought I was shocked at how daring and “cool” he’d been as a kid.

“Me and my mates did it a few times,” Dad said. “What a laugh, right? Tried to get some girls to come too but we didn’t stand a chance.”

Dad was quiet for a few moments, lost in his memory. His smile looked real. Then he remembered he was a dad.

“But I don’t want you getting any ideas and going there, OK?” he said. “The place is a death trap.”

I shook my head and tried not to let all my hidden thoughts scroll down my face.

“They’ve knocked the cottage down anyway,” I said. “Total bulldozer carnage. That’s what Rory was saying this morning.”

It was Dad's turn to look shocked. "Is that right?" The glint of a memory in his eye vanished as he frowned and stared into his coffee mug. "About time the council did something about it, I suppose. But just another part of my life gone, right? Another part of me just bulldozed away. It makes me wonder how the hell I'm still here." Dad lifted his guitar off his lap as if it was heavy and uncomfortable, leaning it up against the table again.

"I'm going to look for the torch," I said. I could feel Dad's mood shifting, changing, darkening. Maybe he'd erupt with anger. Maybe he'd burst into tears. I didn't want to be around either way.

Before I could go, Dad rattled his plastic bottle of painkillers at me. "Get these open for me first, will you?" He tossed me the little bottle. His aim was off and I fumbled it, dropped it. Dad tutted at me. Because it was my fault, clearly.

Picking up the bottle, I noticed the hack and scrape marks around the childproof seal. Dad couldn't get a proper grip with his damaged hands and had been trying to cut the top off with a knife instead. He must have been getting desperate. I didn't recognise the brand on the label.

"Have you run out of the ones the doctor gave you?" I asked.

Dad scowled at me. "She never gives me enough. You know that."

I'd learned the hard way not to try telling him he wasn't meant to eat them like Smarties.

I unscrewed the childproof cap and handed the pill bottle back to him. Dad shook out three tablets and swallowed them with the last dregs of his coffee. He only ever drank coffee because he claimed alcohol messed with his tablets. He stood up and refilled the kettle.

"I'm at work this afternoon," Dad said. "I'll tell the boss you'll be popping round to see his lad before the week's out." It was a challenge. He was daring me to argue.

But I nodded.

"And I want this place looking respectable for when your sister gets here," Dad said.

I nodded again. Even though it was an impossible task.

Dad reached up to the old portable stereo on the shelf and whammed the volume up. Extra loud.

CHAPTER 7

Overnight

Rory and me cycled silently and secretly along the village streets as the sun went down. We went the long way and doubled back on ourselves. We didn't want anybody seeing where we were really going or wondering about the rucksacks on our backs. Once beyond the village we got off the roads and stuck to the farm tracks between the fields.

"Where did you tell your mum you were going?" I asked Rory.

"Said I was camping in your back garden," he replied.

"I told my dad I was camping in yours," I said.

And we grinned at each other's sneakiness.

"I've been dead nervous all day that someone else might have found the den," I said.

"Me too," Rory said. "But I've got a plan for hiding the trapdoor. I'll show you when we get there."

We pedalled faster.

It was nine o'clock when we reached the edge of Skelter Woods. We had at least another hour before it got fully dark. As soon as we got close, it was obvious no one had messed with the trapdoor. We wheeled our bikes a bit deeper into the woods to keep them hidden.

I crouched down next to the trapdoor and brushed all of the mud and leaves away. I was still worried about the ring handle sticking up and being easy to spot. I'd found a screwdriver in our shed when I'd been looking for the torch. I reckoned I could take the handle off if we needed to.

"So what's your plan?" I asked Rory.

He grinned and looked proud of himself as he held up a tube of superglue. "I'm gonna glue branches onto the trapdoor. So even when we're down there and the door's closed it'll stay camouflaged."

"And that glue sticks branches to metal, does it?" I asked.

"Totally. I googled it."

So we grabbed twigs and leaves and a couple of thicker branches. When Rory was done gluing, I had to admit it looked pretty good. Maybe I wouldn't need to take the handle off after all.

"As long as you haven't glued the trapdoor shut," I said.

Rory looked worried and yanked it open quickly. "Phew."

"I was only joking," I said.

"I knew that," he lied. He looked down into the den. "You got a torch, right?"

I clicked it on, shining it right in Rory's eyes, making him squint and duck.

"Very funny," he said.

"I had to put in new batteries but it works great," I told him.

He nodded. "I can tell."

I dropped my rucksack into the den, listening to the soft thump when it hit the ground. Then I followed it down the ladder. When Rory climbed down, he closed the trapdoor very, very gently after him. Then opened it again. Closed it. Then opened it.

"Just checking," Rory said.

My torch's beam was a fuzzy cone of light.

"Definitely darker than before," Rory said.

"Scared?" I asked.

"Only of ghosts of people with shotgun holes in their head."

"Is that one there?" I shouted, pointing at the old and shabby armchair.

Rory swore and spun around to see. "Where?" he said. Then he swore at me when I laughed at him.

I balanced my torch on one of the rungs of the ladder so that it lit up as much of the den as possible.

"So what do you want to do all night?" Rory asked.

"I don't really want to do anything," I said. "I reckon just being here, somewhere no one else knows about, is just brilliant and amazing anyway."

Rory tipped his rucksack upside down. Everything came spilling out – his sleeping bag, his Switch, packets of M&Ms, Haribo, Skittles, four cans of Coke and a deck of playing cards. I also spotted something else.

"You brought pyjamas?" I asked.

"No."

"What are they then?" I pointed at the pale blue PJ leg poking out from under his sleeping bag.

"My mum must have done it when she packed all the sweets," Rory said. He blushed in the torchlight and stuffed the offending item back into his rucksack. "What did you bring?"

"My sleeping bag," I said.

"Is that all?"

I didn't want to say that we didn't have cupboards stuffed with sweets and Coke at my house. Or that Dad packing me anything was as likely as aliens landing in the village.

"Do you reckon we can get a phone signal down here?" Rory asked.

"You did this morning," I said. "But I'm not going to have mine on anyway."

"Why not?"

"You're the only one who ever messages me and you're here."

"I've got to keep mine on because of my mum," Rory said. "What if your dad wants to get in touch with you?"

I shrugged.

Rory shrugged too.

We took the thick woollen blankets from the wooden chest and spread them on the ground. We sprawled on them with the sweets and cans of Coke between us.

"You know what this reminds me of?" Rory asked. "Remember years and years ago your dad always took us on picnics with your sister up Given Hill? He'd make salt 'n' vinegar and prawn cocktail crisp sandwiches, and always filled your packed lunchbox with loads of sweets. Your mum went mad at him every time for not taking any fruit or healthy stuff. And your dad always said his picnics weren't meant to be healthy.

"Last time we went he took his old CD player, didn't he?" Rory went on. "And he taught us how to play air guitar." Rory waggled his fingers like he was holding an imaginary guitar as if to prove it. "You remember that?"

"You're right," I said. "It was years and years ago."

"He's the only person I know who even still listens to CDs," Rory said. "Why don't you tell your dad about Spotify?"

"Because he doesn't want to know," I said. And I didn't want to think about Dad or any of those good times that were long disappeared.

So Rory and I spent the night in the den talking and joking – being us. I let Rory beat me at *Mario Golf* and *Super Smash Bros* on his Switch. He ate all the Haribo; I ate all the M&Ms.

Rory sometimes checked his phone just in case ... But less and less as the night went on. We felt daring and secret. We tried to spook the other one out by pretending we could hear footsteps above us. But we didn't believe each other because we knew the den was too hidden, too secret. And only we knew about it. And only we dared be here, in the middle of the night, on our own.

Who else in the whole world anywhere was doing what we were doing? Just us – best friends.

I didn't think about my dad, even when I used Rory's cards to teach him how to play poker (forgetting that it had been Dad who'd taught me).

We used the leftover Skittles for betting – oranges were worth £10 million, purples worth £50 million. Sometimes we whispered in the dark. Other times we posed or leaped or shrieked around the den in the darkness. Then roared with laughter at the weird, spooky, goofy faces we pulled in the flash photos we took on our phones.

"Starting with the letter A," Rory said, "you've got to go through the whole alphabet saying who you fancy most whose name begins with that letter. I'll start. Alison Tully from Year 10."

"Bethany Munro," I said.

"Mrs Chilton," Rory said.

"What? The Geography teacher?"

And when Rory nodded, I howled with laughter.

It was 2 a.m. by the time we made it all the way to Z. Rory was yawning, making me yawn too. My torchlight was beginning to fade. I was going to need lots of long-life batteries if I was going to keep coming here for the rest of the summer.

It was warm enough in the den that we didn't need to be inside our sleeping bags, so we lay on top of them. We didn't want to use the saggy, grubby bed and were happy on the floor. I switched my torch off.

"This is awesome, isn't it?" Rory said. I couldn't see him in the pitch-dark but I knew him so well I could picture his beaming grin. "Totally awesome – right, Marshall? Totally."

"The best," I agreed.

"Something new, amazing and different," Rory said.

In the underground dark I could sense the closeness, squareness, solidness of the walls around me. But I wasn't worried or scared. Me and Rory were filling the den. Us, our jokes and our friendship. The darkness here was all ours. At home my house always felt full to the brim with Dad's darkness.

I heard Rory begin to snore.

Was there a way I could stay here more often? How could I escape my dad for more than one single night? He wouldn't miss me. How easy would it be to spend the rest of the summer down here?

CHAPTER 8

My Den

Rory's phone woke us. The sound of booming, blasting Napalm Death in the pitch-black would wake anyone up totally bloody quickly.

It was his mum. Rory grabbed for his phone in a panic while I managed to switch the torch on. The beam was dim and the batteries weak but not completely dead yet. Rory told his mum he was sorry three times, four times, as he fought with his sleeping bag. He was trying to stuff it into his rucksack. He looked like he was trying to fit a duvet into a milk bottle.

"I'm coming now," Rory said into his phone. "Don't worry. Stop worrying. I said I'm on my way, didn't I?"

I yanked his sleeping bag off him and rolled it up small so that it would fit back in his rucksack.

When he'd finished the call, Rory said, "I promised Mum yesterday that I'd be home for nine."

"It's only five past," I said.

"I dare you to call her back and tell her that," Rory snapped at me. "You know exactly what Mum's like. She's a control freak."

"At least she's not a loser like my dad," I said.

I was amazed we'd slept so well and so long. I guessed it was the complete dark and silence. No morning light creeping around curtains. No Dad boiling the kettle or flushing the loo. No breakfast microwave beeping.

"Come on, come on," Rory said, already scurrying up the ladder, dragging his rucksack after him. "Hurry up."

For a split second I wondered what would happen if the trapdoor was stuck shut. But Rory shoved it open. He didn't even pause to peek and see if there was anyone around up there, just scrambled out into the sunshine.

I was close behind but I left my sleeping bag and the torch down inside. Popping my head out into the morning sun made me blink and squint. It felt even hotter than yesterday already.

I climbed out and closed the trapdoor. Even in daylight Rory's camouflage looked good. But I was still worried about the ring handle sticking up under the glued-on branches. And we could open the trapdoor without it. So I squatted down and set to work with my screwdriver while Rory got our bikes from further back in the woods. His first, then mine.

"Do you reckon your mum will let you come back tonight?" I called.

"Not two nights in a row," Rory said. "Maybe next week?"

I supposed I'd already guessed that would be his answer. I'd already known I might have to get used to spending most nights alone in the den. All I needed was a pile of long-life torch batteries and better food than Haribo and Skittles, then I reckoned I'd be fine. Maybe I'd even teach myself chess or read one of the books while sitting in the armchair.

Rory brought my bike over and watched me struggle to unscrew the handle. Like everything else it was hard, tight, stuck with age.

"Last night was brilliant," Rory said. "I mean it. Totally awesome."

"Told you it would be."

"But, listen, Marshall, right, I was thinking. Just think how maybe even more brilliant it could be if we let Sam and Trev come."

I tried to ignore him. I wanted to keep my cool. He couldn't be serious. I couldn't budge the handle.

Rory laid my bike on the ground and got on his own, rocking it underneath him. "They're still my friends," he said. "And Trev must have said sorry to you like a hundred times. It used to be brilliant when we all hung around together."

I swore at the stuck handle, or maybe at Rory. "I don't want anything to do with Sam and Trev," I said. "Why would I? They're not *my* friends any more."

"But they used to be," Rory said. "We all used to be. And—"

I jumped to my feet. "Used to be. Exactly. Until Trev broke my nose. You remember he did that, yeah?" I clenched the screwdriver in my fist.

Because if Rory said the fight between me and Trev had been my fault, then maybe I'd ... I'd ...

"It happened months ago and was just sort of a mess-up anyway," Rory said, reversing his bike away a couple of steps from me. "Nothing dead serious, right?"

After the fight between me and Trev, I remembered going home to Dad with blood and snot and tears everywhere. I'd walked in the front door and Dad saw me and he'd held up his scarred hands. "When it hurts as much as these," he'd told me, "then maybe I'll give a damn."

"Maybe you thought it was nothing *dead serious*," I said to Rory. "But it was Trev who was going around calling my dad a loser."

Rory rolled his eyes. "He only said it cos you said it first. You're always calling your dad a loser. You even said it ten minutes ago."

I could feel myself getting angry. It was like I had lava in my belly, getting hotter and hotter, nearly ready to erupt. "He's my dad, so I can say what I want about him. People like Trev need to keep their mouths shut." I pointed the sharp end of the screwdriver at Rory, warning him.

"And you hit Trev first anyway," Rory said.

"Because he wouldn't keep his mouth shut," I replied.

"Trev was trying to be on your side," Rory said. "He was agreeing with you. He was being your mate."

"Yeah, well, now he's on your side, isn't he?" I felt so betrayed by Rory it was almost as painful as a broken nose. I picked up my bike. "It never stopped you from being friends with him and Sam."

"When we were gaming yesterday," Rory said, "both Trev and Sam said that the four of us should get back together. Cos it was always a good laugh when we all hung around together. And if we showed them our den—"

"*My* den," I spat.

Rory was confused. "What?"

"It's *my* den," I said again. "And maybe I don't even want you coming here any more." I jabbed the screwdriver at him, close to his face. "I mean it – stay away."

"As if," he said. "Shut up, Marshall. Why are you being such a dick?"

I didn't answer. I lashed out with the screwdriver. I stabbed it down on his bike's front tyre and burst it. The bang was massive.

I didn't wait to see Rory's reaction. I rode away, fast, without looking back.

CHAPTER 9

Laney Quiet

I pedalled fast and hard all the way home. I felt both angry and guilty, and tried to burn the feelings off with speed and sweat. But I felt hurt and stupid too. So I pedalled faster and harder.

It was all Rory's fault, wasn't it? I didn't care if he had to walk all the way home from the den and got into trouble with his mum, did I? He shouldn't have said what he'd said. No way did I ever want Sam and Trev knowing about the den. Rory was a traitor. And by the time I got home, I'd convinced myself that I was totally, completely, 100 per cent right to have done what I'd done.

I saw my sister's little orange car parked outside our house and it made me smile. She must have left her flat in Lincoln early this morning to get here. I dropped my bike on its side in the garden and went in the front door.

No music meant Dad was still in bed. I left my rucksack in the hall and went straight to the kitchen. Laney was sitting at the table where Dad had been sitting yesterday. But she had a cup of weird-smelling green tea in front of her rather than pitch-black coffee. Laney was wearing a plain white T-shirt but her short hair was dyed the same bright orange as her car.

We grinned at each other and she jumped up to give me a hug. Laney was still taller than me. I'd always thought as I got older I might catch her in height, but not so far. And she was the best hugger I knew. Both arms pulling me in, wrapping me up full and tight – there was no escape.

"Missed you," Laney said in my ear, still not letting me go.

I nodded against her shoulder. I wished she knew how much I missed her too.

Laney let me go. A bit too soon for my liking but I didn't say so. She sat back down and nudged a chair out with her foot for me to sit with her.

"I got here late yesterday," Laney said. "Dad was at work and you were out. You don't answer your phone these days, do you?"

"Me and Rory camped in his back garden," I said. Lying to Dad was a necessity but lying to Laney made me feel lower than low.

She raised one of her perfect eyebrows. "So why does Rory's mum think you camped here? She called about ten minutes ago asking if Rory had left yet." Laney leaned forward as if telling me a secret. "Apparently Rory's not answering his phone now either." She waggled both of her eyebrows at me.

"Did you grass us up?" I asked.

Laney was offended. "You know me better than that," she said. "Rory's mum sounded like she was all ready to come round and pick him up but I managed to put her off. I hope he's as good as me at lying under pressure or you're both screwed."

"As long as you don't tell Dad," I said.

"What, that you and Rory pulled the classic sleepover switch on him?" Laney shook her head. "He told me you were camping when he got home last night, before all of the obvious arguments started. But you can't blame me for feeling a bit worried after Rory's mum called. I was going to give you another half hour this morning before I sent out a search party. You're not going to tell me where you were?"

I didn't like that Laney sounded as if she was interrogating me. She was brilliant and I loved seeing her. Yet it was only a few times each year that she came around. After what had happened with Rory, I didn't know whether or not I wanted to tell her about the den. It was still *my* den and I didn't want to tell *anyone* about it. A big part of me was beginning to wish even Rory didn't know.

"Thanks for not grassing us up," I said.

"It's what big sisters are for." Laney took a gulp of her stinky tea. "But we're also meant to worry about little brothers too. If you're not going to say where you've been all night, that's fine. I can live with it. But tell me you're doing OK. Honestly. Seriously."

That was easy. Because I honestly, seriously was doing OK – now I had the den and could go there any time that I wanted. No lie needed. So I nodded and grinned.

Laney nodded and grinned too.

"Cup of tea?" she said.

I shook my head. "No, thanks."

She frowned. "No, I'm saying I want one. I'm not here to be you and Dad's servant." She held up her empty cup. "Put the kettle on."

I did as I was told.

"Mum says hi," Laney said. "She sent you a present. I put it in your room for you. Have you spoken to her yet this week?"

"We talked on Tuesday." But I hadn't been able to think of much to say.

Laney was always good at having lots to say. As I filled the kettle, she started telling me about the jobs she was applying for now that she'd nearly finished uni. I asked her if it was easy to get a job with orange hair. She said she was so damn awesome she'd get a job if she had no hair whatsoever. I believed her. The kettle was just about boiled when Dad walked into the kitchen and killed our conversation dead.

We both went quiet and watched him. Who knew which Dad he was going to be this morning?

Dad was blurry eyed, already smoking. His long hair was a ratty, greasy mess. The first thing he did was reach up to the old portable stereo on the shelf and switch his music on. He used the just-boiled water to make himself a mug of coffee as black as Batman's shadow.

Laney sighed. "That was meant for me," she said.

Dad looked confused.

"Never mind," she said.

I refilled the kettle for her.

Dad seemed annoyed that Laney was sitting in his usual chair. He dragged another one out from the table and slumped down.

"Couldn't sleep," Dad said. "Bad night."

The room had become full of him. He was a heavy, looming thundercloud filling the air around us. I wanted to open a window and let an easy breeze inside. Or maybe a gusting wind that could blow Dad all the way back upstairs again. Whenever he was around, everything became about him.

"I told Tom Crikey you'd be round to play with his lad Greg sometime this week," Dad said to me.

"I'm thirteen," I said. "I don't *play* any more."

"You play computer games, don't you?" Dad said.

"No, we *game*."

Dad puffed his cheeks out, letting smoke curl from his nostrils. He was a simmering dragon getting ready to burn. "If you say so," Dad said. He drank his scorching-hot coffee.

"Are you choosing Marshall's friends for him now?" Laney asked.

Dad stared at her through half-closed eyes. "I don't see why they can't all play – *game* – together," he said.

"Is Greg Crikey still as big as a gorilla?" Laney asked. "Even when he was younger he looked like someone who pulled the wings off birds for fun."

"Don't be ridiculous," Dad said. "Greg's lonely, that's all. And I can sympathise with that."

"Maybe we should get some of your old friends round to see you," Laney told Dad.

He scowled at her.

"I'm not being funny," she said. "Honestly, I think it could be good for you to see some of your—"

"And you'd know what's good for me now, would you?" Dad said. "You're here about five minutes and already you're clever enough to start deciding what's good for me. I'm so glad I brought up such a genius daughter."

Laney got to her feet and pushed me out of the way as she grabbed the kettle. She hissed something under her breath.

"What was that?" Dad asked.

Laney poured the water for her tea, ignoring him.

Dad hammered a twisted fist down on the table top, making his coffee mug slop. The pain it caused lit up Dad's eyes and he bellowed over his music, "What – did – you – *say*?"

With her back to him, Laney said loud and clear, "*Mum* brought me up." Then she turned to stare him in the eye. She was so much braver than me. "Because you either weren't around or you were too busy feeling sorry for yourself."

I was scared Dad was going to explode in thunder and lightning. Or maybe even burp flames and burn my sister up right where she stood. Maybe if he had a screwdriver in his hands he'd burst her open like a bike tyre. I got ready to run. But he stared down at his hands on the table and took a big, shuddery breath.

It was like a switch inside Dad had been flipped. Instead of thundering or flaming, he began to cry. Silent tears but they shook his whole body.

Laney closed her eyes and let out a long, slow, painful sigh. "Why don't you go see what present Mum sent you?" she said to me. She sat down at the kitchen table again. "I'll talk to Dad."

I disappeared sharpish, more than happy to let Laney do all of the eggshell treading for the day. I wondered how soon it would be before I could get back to the den again.

CHAPTER 10

Traitor

Batteries
Another torch?
Pillow
Bottles of water

I sprawled on my bed writing a list of everything I thought I was going to need at the back of an old Maths exercise book. The "present" Mum had sent was a brand-new pair of expensive jeans. They were too small for me. I supposed it was difficult to know how tall anyone was when you only saw their top halves on a computer screen.

I was itching to get back to the den but Laney had ordered me to stay home. She and Dad had spent all morning talking (and arguing) in the kitchen. But then she'd said she'd cook dinner for the three of us tonight.

Laney hadn't been happy when she realised she had to go out to the supermarket to buy the ingredients she needed. So she'd told me to keep an eye on Dad. This was the easiest job in the world because even though it was only three in the afternoon, he'd fallen asleep at the kitchen table.

All I'd done was creep downstairs and put Dad's smouldering cigarette out. I'd left his music playing because turning it off might have woken him up. He'd held his guitar in his lap looking a bit like a little kid with a teddy bear.

Deodorant
Mouthwash (unless I use bottled water to clean my teeth)

Should I take extra clothes? I had to figure out how often I was planning on coming back home to stock up. And how little could I be around before Dad began to notice? If he ever did notice ...

New lock

I reckoned I wanted to be able to lock myself inside the den. No way did I want anybody surprising me in the middle of the night. I was planning on fixing a bolt or padlock on the underside of trapdoor. But I realised I was also going to need a lock on the outside too. I didn't want anybody getting in when I wasn't there either.

Lock x 2

I decided I'd sneak out to the shed later. I wanted to rummage through the piles of old junk in there to see if I could find anything useful.

My phone burped loudly on the bed next to me. It was the most annoying sound I'd downloaded and it let me know it was Rory sending a text.

I tried to ignore it, telling myself I wasn't interested in anything Rory had to say. Even if he was saying sorry and begging to be friends, I didn't care. But the burps wouldn't stop. My phone was a burping machine gun. And when I gave in and read the texts, they were nothing but strings of swear words. It was all of the most offensive words Rory knew. And some extra ones he'd invented too.

Rory even threatened to tell his mum exactly where we'd spent last night but I knew he'd never dare. Rory was a traitor for wanting to tell Sam and Trev about the den. But no way did I believe he'd risk being grounded by his mum.

Rory's constant texting, and my phone's burping, was getting on my nerves. I switched my phone to silent just as he sent a photo. And then it was me who was shouting the most offensive words I knew.

The photo was from inside the den. It was dark and shadowy but his phone's flash was bright. Rory was looking at the camera with a massive smug grin. I could see the old armchair behind him. And sitting in the armchair, squeezed up together and leering at me, were Sam and Trev.

The shock of Rory's betrayal was like a sledgehammer to my guts.

I was hurt and I was scared too. What if *they* locked *me* out?

Laney wasn't back from the supermarket but I couldn't wait for her. I charged downstairs, not caring if I woke Dad. My bike was still on its side in the garden. I picked it up and ran to get some speed up before I jumped on and raced away down the road. I had another list in my head. A short one that I didn't need to write down.

I have to get to the den.

I have to get them *out* of my den.

I have to get someone to help me do it.

I got to the edge of the village but didn't follow the narrow track that led to Skelter Woods and the den. Instead, I rode as fast as I could towards Crikey's Dog Hotel and hoped Greg was home.

CHAPTER 11

Sides

The Dog Hotel was further out from the village than Skelter Woods and I was puffing for breath by the time I got there. I turned off the main road and cycled up the old, cracked runway. On each side were the large hangars that used to house fighter planes. They had been converted into kennels when Mr Crikey bought the place before I was born.

Dad had worked at Crikey's for the past few years but I'd never actually been here before. And I'd never been close friends with Greg. We sat together at the back of the class in English with Mrs Cornick but the rest of the time we more or less ignored each other.

Not friendly or unfriendly, Greg was quiet enough at school to come across as strange and alone. He was also big enough to never get picked on by mouthy bullies. I knew it was a risk going to Greg for help and asking him to be on my side against Rory, Sam and Trev. I just didn't think I had any better choice.

The afternoon was still sunny and the heat felt low and thick. There were three huge, arched hangars on each side of the long runway. Dad had told me that inside each hangar were fifteen kennels, and each kennel had its own yard space for the dog.

Owners liked sending their dogs here, Dad said, because their pampered pooches had loads of space and weren't kept cooped up in small cages. But I also knew many people in our village hated the Dog Hotel because of all the noise. As I cycled between the hangars, the dogs' barking was louder than I'd ever heard it before. I could also smell them.

A stocky man wearing wellies walked out of one of the hangars. He carried a dripping hosepipe and I guessed he'd been cleaning out some of the kennels. His bald head was shiny in the sun and he shaded his eyes to watch me. Then he waved, smiling. It was Tom Crikey, Greg's dad and my dad's boss, so I waved back. But I didn't stop and kept going all the way to the top of the runway and the old officer barracks. This was Greg's house.

I leaned my bike beside the red-brick porch and rang the doorbell. It was a *bonger* rather than a *dinger*. I was impatient and rang it again after only about half a minute. I was even about to ring it a third time but then Greg opened the door.

Maybe Laney had been being cruel when she called Greg a gorilla. Cruel to gorillas anyway. His hair looked like it had been chewed short by one of the dogs rather than cut by a barber. He was thirteen, same as me, but already had a bit of a dark moustache and bristly sideburns. His greasy, spotty face looked surprised to see me. But only for a second or two.

"My dad said you might turn up," Greg grunted. "Didn't know it was today you were coming." He didn't sound pleased. He didn't sound annoyed either. Greg turned to lead me into his house and I saw he was holding an Xbox controller. "What games do you like?" he asked.

I'd been trying to think of the best way to get him to agree to join my side against Rory. I knew I had to tell him about the den to do it.

"I don't want to game," I said. "I need you to help me. Have you heard of Skelter Cottage?"

He looked at me and the surprise stayed glued to his face this time. "Yeah, course I have," he said. "I used to go there all the time."

"Did you know they've knocked it down?" I said. "Total bulldozer carnage."

He nodded again. "I watched them do it. Dad made me sandwiches and I climbed a tree so I could see everything. Probably the best thing I've ever seen."

Now Greg was the one surprising me. But I said, "Did you know about the bomb shelter underneath?"

"What bomb shelter?" he asked.

I smirked, knowing I was telling him exciting news he knew nothing about. "I reckon it's a bomb shelter," I said. "But it could be an old coal bunker or even just a basement. But it's probably the best thing *I've* ever seen."

"You're lying," Greg said.

"I swear, straight up. Me and Rory found it and we stayed in it last night. Slept there. Underground. All night."

Greg grinned so wide I think it popped a couple of the biggest yellow zits on his cheeks. He tossed his controller onto a small table by the door and pushed past me. "I wanna see it."

"Wait," I said. "Just a minute. Me and Rory found it but now Rory's told Sam and Trev about it." I showed him Rory's photo on my phone. There were more texts (two from Laney and loads from Rory), which I ignored.

Greg peered at the photo, examining it, still not fully trusting that the den was true.

"It was my den too and they've stolen it," I said. "So I need you to help me kick them out. We could get locks for the trapdoor and keep it just for us."

I wasn't telling him the whole truth, maybe. But if Greg helped keep Rory, Sam and Trev out of the den, then I supposed I'd allow him to use it now and again. Although I knew I'd keep hold of the keys to any locks.

"I thought they were your mates," Greg said.

"So did I."

Mr Crikey came striding towards us along the runway. He was even taller than his son. No zits but a thicker moustache. His wellies *thokked* and slapped as he walked.

"You heading out, boys?" Mr Crikey's accent was as strong as the ancient locals who'd been living around here since forever. "Good on you for getting the lazy layabout moving." Mr Crikey winked at me. "Fresh air will do Greg a world of good."

I didn't really know how to answer, so just shrugged.

"How's your dad doing today?" Mr Crikey asked. "Enjoying his day off?"

I shrugged again. But I knew I needed some kind of polite answer, so said, "My sister's come to visit."

"Aye, that's right. Your dad said she was coming. He was looking forward to it. I know he misses her plenty."

This was news to me.

"Marshall says there's a secret bomb shelter under Skelter Cottage," Greg said.

I felt my heart sink. Did nobody know the meaning of "secret" any more?

"Is that right?" Mr Crikey said. His grey eyebrows almost climbed all the way up his shiny bald head.

"It was Marshall's den," Greg went on. "But he says some other kids from school have stolen it and won't let him in any more. Even though it was Marshall that found it in the first place."

"Well, that ain't right, is it?" Mr Crikey said.

"So I'm going with him to help kick them out," Greg said.

I was both amazed and terrified by the conversation. How could Greg tell his dad so much? And why wasn't his dad forbidding him from getting involved? Or stopping him from going somewhere that should be out of bounds and even dangerous?

"You haven't swilled out all the kennels yet, have you?" Greg asked.

Mr Crikey hooked a thumb at the nearest hangar. "Just that one to go."

"Is it all right if me and Marshall make some bombs?" Greg said.

"Bombs for a bomb shelter?" Mr Crikey replied. The father and son laughed with each other at a joke I didn't understand.

Greg grinned his zit-popping grin again. "Thanks, Dad." He strode across the runway towards the nearest hangar. "Come on," he called back to me. "This is the best plan ever."

All I could do was follow. I had to run to keep up.

"Back home before it's dark," his dad shouted after us.

CHAPTER 12

Bombs Away

Greg carried our bombs in a Tesco shopping bag. He'd hung the bag over his handlebars and it swung and swayed as we bounced along the farm track on our bikes. I thought it was a brilliant idea. I also thought it was a terrible idea. And I felt like there was no turning back whatever I thought as I cycled along next to an excited Greg.

The sunlight was casting long shadows by the time we made it to the edge of Skelter Woods. Before we could see the trapdoor, we could hear the voices. Rory, Sam and Trev. The three of them were down in the den with the trapdoor flung wide open. It was impossible to miss if anybody wandered by on the farm track. What was the point of Rory's camouflage of branches if they kept the door open?

Greg and I left our bikes in the long grass to one side of the farm track. We sneaked across the bare, dry mud ground where Skelter Cottage used to stand. As Greg was so tall, he wasn't the sneakiest person in the world. Luckily Rory, Sam and Trev were talking too loud in the den to be able to hear his clomping size 10s.

Greg carried the Tesco bag. Inside were twenty smaller paper bags, wrapped up like little packets of disgustingness. The paper bags were thin – easy to rip and burst. Greg had wanted to make more packets but I'd convinced him that twenty was plenty. We'd been taking so long making them, I'd thought we'd never even get to the den in time.

"We could just dump the bombs on top of them," Greg whispered.

I shook my head. "I don't want the den being totally ruined."

We got flat on our bellies, the same as me and Rory had when we'd first found the trapdoor. We squirmed closer to be able to peer down inside.

"It's awesome," Greg said. "And nobody even knew about it."

"Hidden underneath for years and years," I whispered, feeling proud to have found it. And happy to forget that Rory had been the one to spot the trapdoor handle in the first place.

Looking down, I could see the top of Trev's head. I'd know his ginger mess of hair anywhere. Trev was lounging sideways in the old armchair with his legs thrown over one of the arms. I couldn't see Rory or Sam yet but could hear them.

"I'm not making it up," Sam said. His voice always made him sound like he had a cold. "We could bring spades with us and dig extra rooms and stuff."

"We could make it massive down here," Rory agreed.

"We could make people pay to see it," Trev said.

"That would be epic," Sam said. "They pay to visit the wishing well in the village, don't they? So why wouldn't they pay to see down here?"

I listened to their stupidity but couldn't believe what I was hearing. They were all dickheads. Their plans to tell the whole village, country, world about my den made my belly churn with that hot lava I knew so well. Even when Trev had called Dad a loser and punched me, I hadn't hated him as much as I hated all three of them right here, right now.

"Get out!" I shouted down through the trapdoor.

The way they jumped and scampered was almost funny. Then there were three nervous faces peering up at me and Greg from the bottom of the ladder.

"Marshall?" Rory said. "What're you—"

"Get out!" Greg bellowed. His voice boomed around the den's walls, twice as loud as mine.

"Who's that?" Sam asked.

"Is that Greg?" Rory sounded confused. "Is Greg with you?" he called up.

"What the hell's Marshall doing hanging around with Greg?" Trev wanted to know.

"Get out! Get out!" Greg bellowed.

I'd told him not to but Greg still dropped one of the little paper-bag bombs down through the trapdoor. It fell fast but the three in the den saw it coming and dodged out of the way. The paper bag exploded its brown muck in a gooey, stinky splash when it hit the ground.

"What is that?" Rory wanted to know.

"It's dog turd," Sam wailed. "God, it stinks."

"Come out or you'll get more," Greg bellowed.

But I held him back and shook my head. "No more in the den," I hissed. "Wait until they come out."

He was already holding a fresh turd-bomb in each hand but he shrugged.

We stood up and backed away from the trapdoor. Greg placed the Tesco bag on the ground carefully, making sure it didn't topple and spill our bombs.

"We won't throw any more if you come out," I called.

They were scared to trust us and I had to call out three more times. Only then did Rory poke his head up from the top of the ladder. He scrambled out in a flash when he saw we were standing far back. Then Trev, then Sam.

I made a show of pulling a turd-bomb out of the Tesco bag. It was warm and squishy in my palm. I didn't dare hold it too tight in case the fragile package burst open.

Rory pushed the trapdoor closed. He stood next to Sam and Trev, squaring off to me and Greg. We faced each other on either side of the trapdoor. Maybe if I'd thought about it, it would have felt weird that I was on Greg's side instead of theirs. But I glared back at them. And I don't think Greg cared whose side he was on.

"What're you doing here?" Rory wanted to know.

"More like what are *they* doing here?" I asked, gesturing at Sam and Trev. "You promised to keep the den a secret."

"That was before you stabbed my tyre," Rory said. "I had to walk home because of you. Do you know how apeshit my mum went? She was this close to getting the police to come looking for me." He held his thumb and finger only a centimetre apart to show just how close. "And she was this close to grounding me for the whole summer." He squeezed his fingers closer still.

"You were well out of line, Marshall." Rory got louder and louder as he shouted at me. "You owe me for a new tyre. I mean it, I want the cash. And I had to google how to mend a puncture too." He couldn't stop himself from jiggling on the spot as he ranted at me.

"It's not like you own it here or anything," Sam piped up in his blocked-nose voice. He was the shortest out of all of us. He wore round glasses that were always wonky on his face. "Who says only you can be here?"

Trev stood next to him. At primary school Trev used to hate his ginger hair and the name-calling it caused. But since we'd started secondary school, Trev had shot up in height, becoming one of the tallest kids in our year. He was more than happy to fight anyone who tried taking the mickey out of him.

Trev jabbed a threatening finger at the turd-bomb in my hand. "If you throw another one of them at me, I'll kick your face in." He meant it.

"Will you kick my face in too?" Greg asked.

"Throw one and find out," Trev replied.

"We won't throw anything if you go," I said. "And don't come back."

"I found it too," Rory said. "You can't stop me from coming here."

"You don't need it," I said.

"What's that supposed to mean?" Trev sneered.

"You don't own it," Sam repeated annoyingly. "You don't own it."

"Maybe it's ours now," Rory said.

"It's not for you," I said. "I'm the one who has to be here."

"What are you on about?" Trev mocked me. "Are you high?"

I was getting hotter with the angry red lava rising inside me. Why couldn't any of them understand? I wanted them gone. But they looked at me like I was some weird saddo who needed their sympathy. And I began to feel embarrassed – because of what I'd just said.

Rory had stopped ranting and hopping. He was staring at me. Maybe he understood? But I hated that look of sympathy in his eye.

"Is this all because you're still in escape-mode?" Rory asked.

He wasn't supposed to look at me when he asked questions like that. So I threw my turd-bomb at him.

It burst its muck across his chest. Rory jumped back and screamed like he'd been shot.

Then, laughing, Greg threw the two bombs he was holding. Trev was too slow to dodge. One bomb missed by a mile but the other exploded against his shoulder, showering him in stink. Trev roared with rage.

I grabbed the Tesco bag from Greg, wanting to dig inside for another bomb. Rory was screaming and shouting. He ran at me. He rammed into me so hard he flung me over, smashing the wind out of me as I hit the ground. I dropped the Tesco bag. I tried to roll away but Rory wouldn't stop.

Greg was too solid for Trev to knock down. So Trev swung wide punches at him. I'd been on the receiving end of a Trev punch and it had hurt. Greg jabbed and slapped back but Trev was faster. Greg staggered and grunted with every punch Trev landed.

Sam shouted, "Stop. Stop it!" from a safe distance.

Rory had the bomb's mess across his chest and splattered around his neck. I tried to roll away but I couldn't get up from under him. I rolled onto the dropped Tesco bag, crushing and bursting the bombs inside.

Rory had his full weight on me, holding me down. The squashed bombs squirted and oozed out of the bag beneath me. It was thick, sticky, smelly, sludgy, slimy, gross. Rory grabbed my forehead and pushed the back of my head into it. I had to knee him in the balls, making him gasp.

At last I pushed him off me. But I had the stench of filthy turd-bomb smeared all the way up the back of my T-shirt and matted in my hair.

I wanted to kill him. But the fight had drained out of me. I got to my feet. I was dripping, stinking.

Trev and Greg had stopped fighting. They stood and stared at me. Trev's mouth hung open. He looked like he might puke.

"Holy shit," Greg said. And laughed.

I was scared I might cry.

Rory panted hard, his face grim. Who knew he had so much of his own lava inside him?

"You deserved it," he said to me. But he looked shocked and pale and I don't know if he meant it.

"Someone's coming," Sam shouted. "Someone's coming."

Maybe we would have carried on fighting if the dog hadn't appeared at the edge of the farm track. It was a black-and-white collie and it bounded towards us, barking. We heard the owner calling for it.

And it was a good excuse for the five of us to all run for our bikes.

We were probably the last thing the dog walker expected to see on his quiet evening stroll. He frowned at us from under his flat cap. But we kept our heads down and faces turned away as we sped past him. We didn't give him a chance to remember what we looked like, all shooting off in different directions like an exploding star.

CHAPTER 13

Laney Loud

It was dark by the time I got home. The stink had become too much for me even before I'd reached the village, so I'd pulled off my T-shirt and chucked it into a bush without even stopping. But I could still smell the turd-bombs in my hair and down the back of my neck. Pedalling faster seemed to blow the worst of the stench behind me, so I pedalled pretty damn fast.

I zoomed through our front gate and didn't even bother to brake. I jumped off my bike and let it crash in a heap in the garden as I ran into the house.

Laney was waiting for me. She came storming along the hall from the kitchen.

"Where the hell ...?" Laney said.

Her eyes bulged. She couldn't believe the state of me.

"Oh my god. Marshall, what's ...?" She screwed up her face in disgust. "What have you ...?"

I shoved past her and sprinted up the stairs two at a time. She didn't stop me. I stank too bad for her to even want to.

She tried calling after me but I ignored her. I was scared I might puke if I stopped moving for even a single second.

I dived straight in the shower. And I made sure the water was scalding.

I opened and completely used up a whole new bottle of shower gel.

I didn't watch what got washed down the plughole. It wasn't too long before I could only smell citrusy shower gel. It felt like I'd been trying not to breathe for hours.

The water began to cool, then go cold. We never had a lot of hot water. I waited until it was like melting icebergs coming out of the shower head before I switched the water off and got out.

When I walked across the landing from the bathroom to my bedroom, I could hear Laney arguing with Dad downstairs. I didn't want either of them coming up here and arguing with me, so I crept into my room and closed my door silently behind me.

I wanted my phone but I realised I'd left it in my jeans, which I'd dumped in the bathroom's laundry basket. I swore at myself. I wanted to know if Rory had sent me more raging messages like earlier. I guessed they were the only kind of messages I'd get from him from now on. Our friendship was totally dead.

But did I care? Not if I still had the den. Total escape.

I was worried about the dog walker. I remembered Rory had closed the trapdoor after he, Sam and Trev had climbed out. But what if the dog walker had got suspicious and nosy? What if his dog had started sniffing around too? I wanted to go back and check everything was still secret and hidden. But I knew there was no way Laney would let me set foot outside the house tonight. She'd rather chain me to my bed, I reckoned.

The need to get my phone was too strong. I was positive there'd be messages flying back and forth. Messages about me, aimed at me.

I got dressed and crept back out onto the landing. I didn't switch the light on. Laney was shouting in the kitchen. Dad was bellowing back. I reckoned they were both louder than his music normally was. I wondered if the neighbours would complain. I sneaked to the top of the stairs and sat in the dark to listen.

Laney shouted, "Don't you get it? You're going to lose him."

"And how would you know?" Dad bellowed back. "You're hardly here."

"It's obvious. Can't you see it? He's already half-gone now."

"He's upstairs, for Christ's sake," Dad shouted.

"And where was he last night?" Laney asked. "You know he wasn't really at Rory's, don't you? But he won't even tell me where he was."

It stung that my sister was grassing me up. First Rory had betrayed me and now Laney.

"And have you seen the state he was in when he got home?" Laney went on, top volume. "I mean, my god. I don't know what the hell he was covered in or how he got that way."

"What do you expect me to do about it?" Dad bellowed back. "Do you think he even listens to me any more?"

Laney's voice dropped so much I had to strain to listen. But her quiet words were deadly sharp. "Then he'll be gone for ever, won't he? Do you want that? Think about it. First Mum, then me, and now Marshall. Help him, Dad. Help yourself."

Tears prickled at the back of my eyes. They surprised me.

I swiped them away. I was too scared to listen to what Dad might answer, so scurried to the bathroom before I would hear. I pulled my jeans out of the laundry basket and dug through my pockets until I found my phone.

Most of the messages were from Sam and Trev. Lots of childish jokes and mouthing-off about what had happened at the den. And stuff about what they were going to do to the den. They'd included me in the messages because they'd wanted to wind me up. It worked.

I scrolled through them, looking for something from Rory. He'd only sent one. It read:

It's our den for ever unless he wants to fight me for it. Just me and him. If he dares to meet me tomorrow at 9. Winner gets the den.

Was he serious?

The rest of the texts were Sam and Trev calling me a chicken, calling me a wimp, calling me a loser.

I'll be there, I texted back. Then I switched my phone off.

When I sneaked back to my bedroom, there was no more shouting from downstairs. All I could hear was Dad's music playing again.

CHAPTER 14

Friend Against Friend

There was a storm overnight. I hadn't slept much, just lay there listening to the rain, and was wide awake early. My thoughts in the dark had been like a line of dominoes toppling, clattering along and racing away. I hadn't been able to slow them down or shut them up.

By the morning the rain was long gone and the sun was already hot through my bedroom window. It was eight o'clock when I heard my sister moving around downstairs and I decided it was time for me to get going.

I hurried to get dressed. Laney had said she'd be heading home to Lincoln today and I didn't want to have to do all of the saying goodbye stuff. I was also still raging at her for grassing me up to Dad, wasn't I? So I climbed out of my bedroom window and dropped down into the garden. I wasn't giving Laney or Dad a chance to stop me, quickly jumping on my bike and speeding towards the den.

Head down against the wind, I went as fast as I could. I'd thought a lot about Rory last night. Two days ago he'd been my best friend. This morning I was going to have to fight him.

Fine. Easy.

I'd win and the den would be mine.

And all of the stuff Laney and Dad had been talking about last night wouldn't matter because I'd have the den to go to.

I leaned right over my bike's handlebars, feeling the wind in my face. The rush of air made me scrunch up my eyes. I rode fast, faster, fastest along the grassy track between the hedges and trees. I slammed up a gear and rammed the pedals round.

I didn't slow down until I reached Skelter Woods. I was worried the dog walker from last night might have found the trapdoor. But as I rode closer it was obvious the clearing at the edge of the trees was undisturbed. Last night's rainstorm had even washed away the remains of the turd-bombs. The camouflaged trapdoor was closed.

I stashed my bike in the trees and went to check the time. Then swore out loud when I realised I'd forgotten my phone. I must have left it in my bedroom as I'd been in such a rush to avoid Laney and Dad and get out of the house. So all I could do was wait. Maybe Rory had chickened out and might have sent some squirming, cowardly text about his mum keeping him home?

But I knew Rory too well. He wasn't a coward. If he made his mind up about something, he stuck with it. I guessed that's why he'd stayed friends with me for so long. Until this morning.

I waited in the shadow of the trees with my bike. After maybe a quarter of an hour, Greg was the first to appear. I hadn't expected him to be here too.

"Hey," I called as I went to meet him. "What are you doing here?"

Greg planted his massive feet down on either side of his bike but stayed sitting on the seat. "Rory told me you and him are going to fight."

"But you're still on my side, right?" I asked.

He shrugged and said, "Didn't know there were still sides."

"So you just came to watch?" I said.

Greg grinned his big, zit-popping grin. "Nothing on telly, is there?"

His grin made me nervous. It was meant to be me versus Rory but he was still friends with Sam and Trev, and maybe even Greg too now. I was truly alone.

Greg dumped his bike and walked over to the trapdoor. He yanked it open and looked inside. "It's so cool," he said. He started to climb down inside. "Don't start the fight without me."

My mouth hung open as I watched him. I was beginning to understand how much I'd been kidding myself. Even if I won this fight, how was I meant to stop anybody else from using the den? The sun felt not just hot but heavy too.

I heard their voices coming along the farm track. Rory, closely followed by Sam and Trev. Seeing the three of them together felt like getting stabbed in the back all over again. Was I going to have to fight everyone?

"You're here then," Rory said. He didn't look nervous or worried about having to fight me. Maybe he was hiding those feelings the same as I was.

"I don't say one thing to people and then do something else," I said. I wanted to feel angry. Fighting would be easier if I had lava in my belly.

Trev got off his bike and sniffed the air. "Can you still smell something?" he asked. He was wearing a cap and his messy ginger hair stuck out from the hole at the back of it.

Sam giggled behind his wonky glasses. He wafted the air from in front of his nose, acting as if it stank.

And that was good. They could wind me up as much as they wanted to because all it did was help stir up the lava inside.

But when I met Rory's eyes, I thought I could tell that he was nervous too. Just a flash of it. But he blinked hard and turned away. We both knew we were going to fight and punch and kick and try to hurt each other. That was exactly what we were here for. We were going to hurt the other one until they gave in. And maybe I'd win. Maybe Rory would have to admit the den was mine. But I'd never get to share it with him again.

It was his fault, I told myself. Rory had betrayed me.

He laid his bike down next to Greg's. "Is Greg in the den?" Rory asked.

I nodded. I was beginning to sweat. Maybe because of the sun, maybe because of the nerves.

"He's not going to help you, is he?" Rory asked.

"I don't need anyone's help," I told him.

Trev and Sam laughed but I didn't get the joke.

Keep laughing, I thought. *Make my lava boil.*

Rory stood facing me. He had his fists clenched and his teeth gritted. He didn't look happy but he looked determined. "This is for my bike tyre," Rory said. "And for getting me in trouble with my mum. And for the turd-bombs."

"You betrayed me first," I said. I clenched my fists too and they felt slick and sweaty.

Rory shook his head. "It's not true and you know it."

"You told them," I said, and pointed at Sam and Trev. I could feel my heartbeat. It was as fast and loud as any of Dad's favourite songs.

"Because they're my friends," Rory replied. "Better friends than you'd ever know how to be."

That hurt, almost as much as a punch. I'd known Rory longer than he'd known either of them. He'd always been my best friend.

Rory hopped from foot to foot and raised his fists. But he was no boxer.

My first instinct was to duck and run. But I made myself stand my ground and raised my own fists. We didn't punch each other. We rammed chests – slamming each other a step or two backwards. It knocked the breath out of me.

"Come on then," I shouted.

"If you dare," Rory shouted.

We waved our fists but didn't use them.

"Come on," I said.

"You come on," Rory replied.

I grabbed the front of Rory's T-shirt. He shoved me away.

He tried to get me in a headlock and I squirmed out of his grasp.

"Come on," I repeated, shouting louder.

"You come on," Rory repeated, shouting even louder.

We threatened each other with our fists.

"If you dare!"

"If you think you're hard enough!"

Rory kicked out at me but missed. I went to shove him backwards but he dodged me easily. We banged chests again, just not as hard, and bellowed in each other's faces.

"Come on then!"

"Any time!"

I glared at him and he swore at me.

"Hit him already," Greg said. He'd popped his head out of the trapdoor. "Go on, smack him." I didn't know if he was talking to me or Rory.

"Hit him," Trev shouted.

"Punch him," Sam joined in.

But all of a sudden I could see that Rory didn't want to fight. That nervous flash in his eye was brighter now. Neither of us truly wanted to fight. We just didn't know how to back down.

We stalked around and around each other with our fists clenched and teeth gritted. We acted like we totally hated each other. We were both panting as if we really were fighting.

"Come on then," I said yet again.

"You come on," Rory replied yet again.

"Car!" Sam shouted. "There's a car."

We all heard it driving up the farm track, its engine getting louder and closer.

I didn't know what to do. Hit Rory, hide, or slam the trapdoor closed on Greg's head? Not that I had time to do anything.

My sister's little orange car drove right up to the edge of the trees.

Rory was as shocked as me. "Is that Laney?" he asked.

All I could do was nod.

Trev and Sam looked confused. They waited to see if we were going to run for it first.

"And your dad?" Rory looked worried, maybe thinking I was going to get my dad to fight him or something. But I was as surprised as he was.

I watched Dad open the passenger-side door and climb out. He nodded at the four of us standing around. His long hair hung loose over his shoulders. He was wearing clean jeans. He noticed Greg's head poking up from the ground and he smiled. Greg hauled himself up the ladder and watched Dad curiously.

Dad was carrying my phone in his crooked right hand and he held it up for us all to see.

"You forgot this," Dad said to me. "I had to read your texts to find out where you'd gone." He sighed, looked at Rory. "Didn't like the sound of a lot of them."

Dad tossed me the phone. I caught it easily.

I turned to look at Laney, who was still sitting in the driver's seat. She mouthed at me, *Stay. Wait*.

Dad reached back into the car and pulled out his old, battered CD player and two carrier bags. He walked towards the trapdoor and Rory, Greg and I stepped to one side to let him pass. Dad placed the CD player on the ground and sat down next to it.

"What is that?" Sam whispered to Trev.

It surprised Dad but then made him laugh. He pressed *play* and the clearing was suddenly full of loud guitars, drums, rhythm, singing, music. Dad tipped one of the carrier bags upside down and out tumbled packets of crisps, a couple of Mars Bars, Snickers, Twix and several cans of Coke. Dad held up a can to Greg, offering it to him.

Greg shrugged, then nodded and took the can from him. He sat down too and cracked it open. Greg took a long, thirsty gulp.

"It's like those picnics we had at the top of Given Hill," Rory said to me.

I didn't answer.

Dad beckoned Sam and Trev to join him, offering them a chocolate bar. They hesitated at first but it was looking like Greg might eat everything by himself, so they hurried over and sat down next to him.

The idea that we'd come here to fight was gone. The tension gone. The anger gone. It had been totally drowned out by the music.

"Can you make me a crisp sandwich?" Rory asked.

"Salt 'n' vinegar or prawn cocktail?" Dad called in reply. He pulled a loaf of bread out of the second carrier bag like a magician yanking a rabbit out of a hat.

Rory whooped with delight and plonked himself down beside the trapdoor. "Both!" Rory said.

The touch on my shoulder startled me but it was only Laney. She'd walked over from her car.

"It's a start, isn't it?" Laney said.

"What's he doing?" I asked her.

"Trying to help," she said.

"Help who?"

"Both you and him," Laney said, and squeezed my shoulder. "Come on." And she led me over to join the circle of friends sitting around the trapdoor.

"Is there really a CD in there?" Sam asked Dad. "Can I see it?"

Trev took his cap off to show his ginger hair. "I love the colour of your car," he told Laney.

"My mum never, ever lets me have crisp sandwiches," Rory said.

Greg tore an empty packet of crisps all the way open and licked the inside foil clean.

"So this is your den, is it?" Dad asked me, peering down into the trapdoor.

I shrugged, nodded and mumbled something Dad didn't hear.

He cupped a bent hand to his ear. "What did you say?" Dad asked.

"Rory found it," I shouted over his music.

CHAPTER 15

Dad's Guitar

I bounced my bike up onto the pavement and through the garden gate. I leaned it up beside the front door and stood for a moment listening. Our house was quiet.

I knew Dad had a shift at the Dog Hotel but I didn't think that it started until later in the afternoon.

Laney had already set off back to Lincoln saying she'd come and visit more often. The hug goodbye she'd given me had been a long one. Dad told her to drive safe. Trev told me how much he fancied her.

Back at the den both Laney and Dad had wanted to look inside. Laney had declared it far too spooky for her, while Dad had been torn – half-parent but also half the kid he once was.

Dad had said, "You know, as the supposed grown-up here, I should be forbidding you all from coming anywhere near this place, shouldn't I? For all sorts of reasons, yeah?"

The five of us had stared at our feet, fidgeted, looked worried and awkward.

"But that would be tricky for everyone, I reckon," Dad had said. "Because then you'd have to sneak here behind my back, wouldn't you? And I'm thinking I'd rather know where you really were if I needed you than have to be guessing all the time. So no more lies, and just promise me you'll all be careful, OK?"

We'd promised. And I didn't know about the others but I'd meant it.

"Can we keep your CD player here?" Sam had asked.

"No way. Get your own," Dad had told him.

Dad and Laney had left, and Greg, Trev and Sam had finished off the Mars Bars, crisps and Coke at the top of the ladder. Me and Rory had climbed back down inside the den. It was so much cooler out of the midday sun.

Greg had called down to us, "So are you two mates again now?"

Rory had looked at me. I'd nodded. "I suppose so," I'd shouted back up.

"Good. Because you're crap at fighting," Greg had boomed.

Rory had slumped back in the old, saggy armchair. The shaft of sunlight from above had made him glow.

"I reckon this summer's going to be the best ever," Rory had said.

I hoped so.

I'd left my four friends at the den. I'd said I'd meet back up with them again later. And now, as I opened the front door and stepped into the house, I repeated under my breath, "I hope so. I hope so."

I still couldn't hear Dad. Maybe he'd gone to work early?

I walked into the kitchen and saw there was Dad's half-drunk mug of coffee on the table and the ashtray was overflowing. The portable CD player was back on the shelf. And Dad's old guitar was leaning up against the wall same as always. Nothing had changed in here.

Still thinking I was alone in the house, I picked up the guitar and sat at the table. It was the first time I'd ever dared touch his guitar. It was heavier than I'd imagined. But smoother and cooler too. It felt good.

I rested the guitar in my lap and plucked at the strings. Then strummed them. Was it meant to sound like that? How could I know if it was even in tune any more? Rory would probably tell me to google it.

Dad walked in. I didn't have time to put his guitar back and don't think I could have looked any more guilty if I'd tried. He stood in the kitchen doorway looking at me, looking at the guitar.

I jumped up. "I'm sorry," I said. "I didn't mean ... I was just ..."

Dad sighed and smiled, then said, "I can teach you how to play if you'd like."

Acknowledgements

With thanks to Lucy Juckes, Catherine Coe, Ailsa Bathgate and all of the wonderful team at Barrington Stoke. Thanks to Jen Cornick for the many cafe chats, and to Steve Brown for giving me the name "Laney". Also to the Sunday Writers' Club members who offered thoughtful feedback on early chapters, and to the Write Magic sprinters for their good company. As ever, biggest thanks and all my love goes to my forever readers, Jasmine and Clara.

Our books are tested
for children and young people by
children and young people.

Thanks to everyone who consulted on
a manuscript for their time and effort in
helping us to make our books better
for our readers.